Cooking Up the Past

Columbus, OH

SRAonline.com

An Open Court Curriculum.

Printed in China.

Send all inquiries to this address:
SRA/McGraw-Hill
4400 Easton Commons
Columbus, OH 43219

ISBN: 978-0-07-608729-7
MHID: 0-07-608729-8

1 2 3 4 5 6 7 8 9 NOR 13 12 11 10 09 08 07

The McGraw-Hill Companies

As soon as the classroom door closed behind them, Karin turned to Geeta.

"Can you believe Mr. Ryan wants us to have an multicultural potluck?" asked Karin.

"I think it could be fun," said Geeta.

"Well, you're lucky," said Karin. "Your family *has* traditional food. Mine doesn't. I'll probably end up bringing tuna noodle casserole! That's my family's idea of traditional food."

"I don't think I've ever had tuna noodle casserole," said Geeta.

"Of course you haven't," said Karin. "It's pretty boring."

Geeta had to admit that tuna noodle casserole did sound kind of boring.

That night at the dinner table, Geeta told her mother and father about the potluck.

"It sounds like an excellent idea," said Geeta's father. "You can learn a lot about other cultures from their food."

"Have you thought about what you want to take to the potluck?" asked Geeta's mother.

"I was thinking maybe palak paneer. I like spinach curry with cheese. I think the kids in my class might like it, too," Geeta said.

“A very good choice,” said her father. “It’s not too spicy. The cheese is like pizza cheese. It’ll be good for people who don’t like a lot of spices.”

“We can make the cheese, or paneer, ourselves,” said Geeta’s mother.

“We’re going to *make* cheese?” said Geeta. “Why can’t we just buy it at the Indian market?”

“I think your teacher wants you to learn about your family traditions as well as the traditions of the other students. We will make the paneer together, just the way my mother and I used to make it when I was your age,” said Geeta’s mother.

The night before the potluck, Geeta and her mother got ready to make the paneer. They poured milk into a pot and heated it on the stove. When the milk started to boil, Geeta's mother took the pot off the stove and added some lemon juice.

"Now we wait for the milk to separate into curds and whey," she explained.

"How long does it take?" asked Geeta.

"About ten minutes," said her mother.

"Ten whole minutes?" Geeta mumbled. "This is going to take forever."

Geeta and her mother sat down at the kitchen table, where her father was reading the newspaper, to wait.

"When my family first came to the United States," her mother said, "we always made our own paneer. We had to make it. There was no place to buy it. There was only a handful of Indian families living here then, and no stores sold the items that were needed for Indian cooking."

"How long ago was that?" asked Geeta.

"We came here in 1974, when I was eleven years old. Your grandfather had been offered a job at the hospital, and the whole family moved here with him. There were one or two other Indian doctors working at the hospital then. It was a good opportunity for him, but it was very difficult for your grandmother," her mother said.

"Why?" asked Geeta. "Couldn't she speak English?"

"Oh, no, that wasn't it," said her mother. "She spoke fluent English. We all did. India was a British colony when your grandparents were born. It didn't gain independence until 1947. Everyone learned English in school. They still do."

She went on, "No, your grandmother didn't have any trouble speaking the language. She found it hard to adjust to a different culture. She was used to living near family and friends who had the same values, customs, and traditions. In this country, everything was different. Some people assumed the newcomers wanted to change their customs, but your grandmother didn't want to change hers. She was determined to keep her Indian customs and traditions and teach her children to do the same."

The timer went off on the stove, and Geeta's mother announced that it was time to strain the milk.

"Let me help you with that," said Geeta's father.

Geeta's mother stretched cheesecloth over the top of a big bowl. Her father carefully poured the milk, which had separated into curds and whey, through the cheesecloth. The curds stayed in the cheesecloth. The watery whey dripped into the bowl. Then Geeta's mother wrapped the cheesecloth around the curds to squeeze out the extra whey.

"Now we need to flatten the cheese so that it's about half an inch thick," said Geeta's mother. "Do you want to do that, Geeta?"

As Geeta worked she said, “Mom, tell me more about Grandma.”

“Your grandmother took great pride in her cooking. She believed that Indian food was the finest in the world. In her opinion, everything else was bland and boring.”

Geeta thought about what Karin had said about the tuna noodle casserole. Then she thought about pizza and cheeseburgers. Those foods were *not* boring.

“Your grandmother did not like American supermarkets, either. She thought they were huge places filled with nothing that was edible. She refused to shop at them,” Geeta’s mother continued. “When we came to the United States, she brought all the spices she needed for her cooking with her. Little bags of spices were tucked everywhere in our trunks and suitcases.”

With elbows propped on the table, Geeta's mother went on with her story. "In less than a year, she had used up all the spices. That's when she got her family and friends back in India to ship spices to her."

Geeta giggled. "You're kidding!"

"Your grandfather didn't really understand it. He thought she was going a little too far, but he never questioned it or tried to stop her. Instead, he tried to be very supportive. Because your grandmother hated American supermarkets so much, he was the one who did the food shopping. Once he came home with a jar labeled 'Indian Curry.' Your grandmother was not happy that he had bought that 'that awful yellow stuff.' It was nothing like her homemade curry."

"Well, you won't use the stuff either," Geeta's father teased.

"That's true," Geeta's mother admitted before returning to her story. "Your grandmother resisted change of any kind. She was very strict with your aunt and me. She was afraid that we would learn American ways, as she put it, and would not follow Indian traditions. We went to a school that had uniforms, and we wore those American uniforms to school. But at all other times, we were forbidden to wear American clothes. We weren't allowed to wear jeans. We weren't allowed to wear sneakers."

Geeta looked down at her own jeans and sneakers.

“But Grandma seems to have changed now,” Geeta said. She thought about all the pizzas she had shared with her grandmother. Geeta also remembered the time her grandmother had taken her to a theme park to ride roller coasters.

“You’re right,” said her mother. “She has changed somewhat. I guess she figured she taught Aunt Daya and me all she knew about Indian customs when we were growing up.” She smiled at Geeta’s father.

With that, Geeta’s mother checked the paneer and declared it ready to go into the refrigerator.

After school the next day, Geeta and her mother continued the preparation of the palak paneer. They soaked the spices. They browned the cheese. They sautéed the onions. They simmered the spinach and potatoes. They grated the fresh ginger. When the dish was done, Geeta and her parents dressed in traditional Indian clothes and headed for Geeta's school.

When they got there, students and parents were gathered in the gymnasium. The hum of conversation and the smell of a mix of interesting foods filled the air. Geeta brought the palak paneer to the potluck table just as Karin was putting her dish there. Geeta looked at Karin's food.

"Is *that* tuna noodle casserole?" asked Geeta. "It looks delicious!"

"No," Karin laughed, "it's fish soup. It's a Norwegian dish. My mom learned to make it from my great-grandmother, who came from Norway. I never even knew I *had* a great-grandmother from Norway! But now I know all about her. She was awesome!"

"The same thing happened to me," said Geeta. "My mom told me things about my grandmother that I never knew before."

"This potluck was a pretty good idea," said Karin.

Geeta agreed, looking down the long table at the colorful and strange foods. She could not wait to dig in!

Vocabulary

fluent (flo͞o´ ənt) (page 8) *adj.* Able to speak effortlessly.

assumed (ə so͞omd´) (page 8) *v.* Past tense of **assume:** To take for granted.

finest (fī´ nəst) (page 10) *adj.* Best; most excellent.

edible (ed´ ə bəl) (page 10) *adj.* Fit or safe to eat.

propped (propd) (page 11) *adj.* Supported by something under or against.

ship (ship) (page 11) *v.* To send by ship, train, truck, or airplane.

Comprehension Focus: Making Connections

1. In what ways is palak paneer like other foods you have eaten? Have you ever tried food from a different culture?
2. What dish would you bring to a multicultural potluck? What other dishes would you like to try?